Elizabeth & Kaylee:
Believe in
your dreams!
Audrey Haag
(Andrea the
Birthday Fairy)
12/01

Audreena

the Birthday Fairy

A book by Stephanie & Scott Sample

Inspired from the concept by Audrey Haag

Based on *The Story of the Birthday Fairy* by Paul Chapin

Creative Publishing international

Very high in the sky, near the sun and the moon,

On the way to the Milky Way

Is a magical cloud where wishes come true;

It's the land where all fairies play.

In this beautiful cloud that is far, far away—

In this place beyond the sun's light

Live mystical fairies, who make us so happy,

And fairies who give us delight.

There's a fairy of sweets—of cookies and candy—

And a fairy who tickles your toes.

There's a bedtime fairy and a fairy of song,

And a fairy who tweaks your nose.

There's a fairy of trees, and she changes the leaves

Every fall from green to bright gold.

The fairy of winter carves up snowflakes from ice

And sprinkles them down when it's cold.

In this place in the clouds, the sky would be dark,

And the fairies would live in the night,

If it weren't for children's bright, happy smiles

That turn the darkness to beautiful light.

For each time a fairy makes small children grin—

When there are giggles and smiles—

A sunbeam of light shines way up to the cloud

And it glows for miles and miles.

On this cloud in the sky is a fairy with dreams

And her name is sweet Audreena.

Her father is Alden, the famous tooth fairy,

Her sisters are Claire and Katrina.

Alden thought his three girls would be tooth fairies like him,

Claire and Katrina both thought so, too.

But Audreena had hopes and dreams of her own—

To make children's wishes come true.

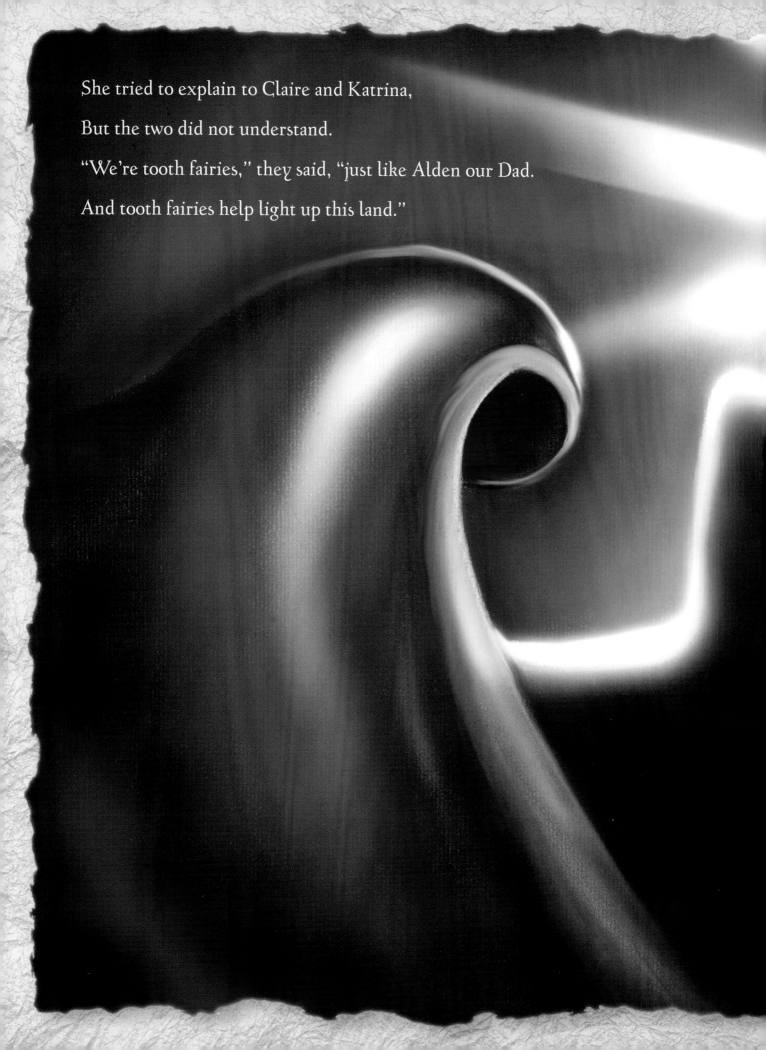

She tried to explain to Claire and Katrina,

But the two did not understand.

"We're tooth fairies," they said, "just like Alden our Dad.

And tooth fairies help light up this land."

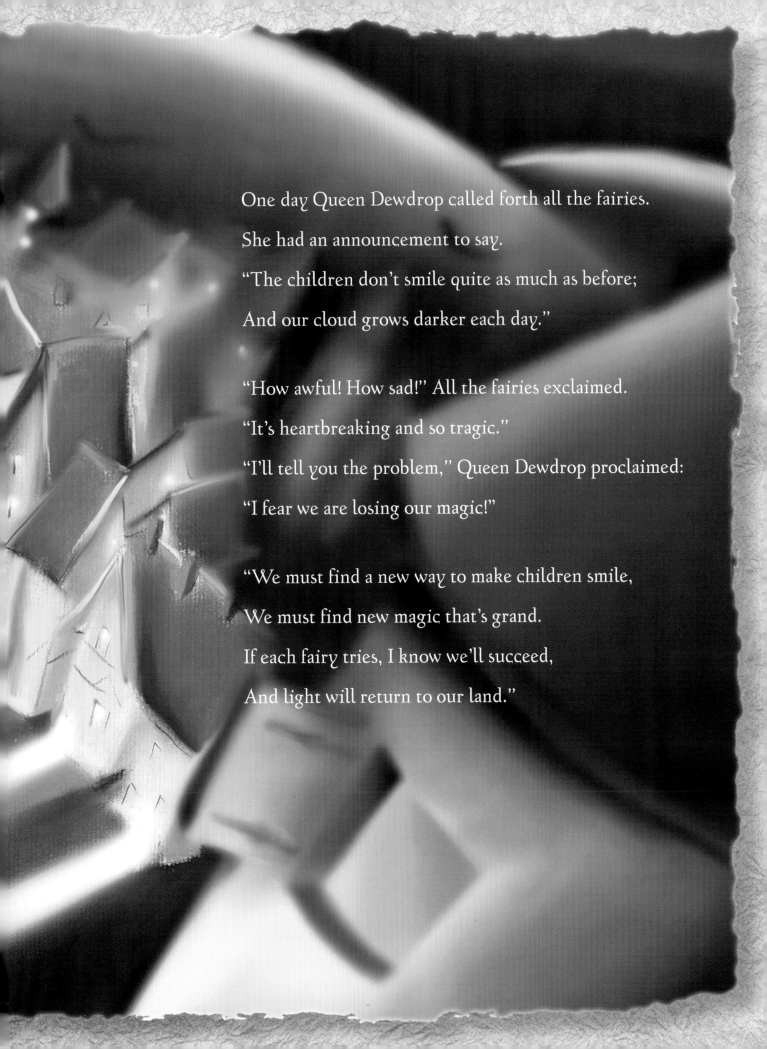

One day Queen Dewdrop called forth all the fairies.

She had an announcement to say.

"The children don't smile quite as much as before;

And our cloud grows darker each day."

"How awful! How sad!" All the fairies exclaimed.

"It's heartbreaking and so tragic."

"I'll tell you the problem," Queen Dewdrop proclaimed:

"I fear we are losing our magic!"

"We must find a new way to make children smile,

We must find new magic that's grand.

If each fairy tries, I know we'll succeed,

And light will return to our land."

Audreena just listened and thought, "How can I help?

I can do it, I just don't know how.

But I know if my dreams are going to come true,

I must find some new magic right now."

While all this was happening in the cloud up above,

Something, too, was happening below.

A young boy named Alex was feeling so sad,

And his eyes had lost all their glow.

For Alex's birthday was the very next day.

He was sure his parents forgot.

Had they made any plans or baked him a cake?

Had his birthday presents been bought?

As he sat in his room feeling lonely and sad,

He wiggled a loose tooth he had.

As he gave it a twist, it wiggled again,

And it popped right out on his bed.

Then Alex's parents called up to his room,

"Hey, buddy, come join us downstairs."

"I'm busy," said Alex, "I just lost my tooth,

But I doubt if anyone cares."

"We think that's great, Alex," both parents exclaimed.

"The Tooth Fairy's going to come."

"I'm sure she'll forget—just like you," Alex said.

"Besides, I think fairies are dumb."

Although Alex said that he didn't believe,

By his pillow he put his tooth.

"I'll stay wide awake, and I'll see who comes in.

By morning I'll know the truth."

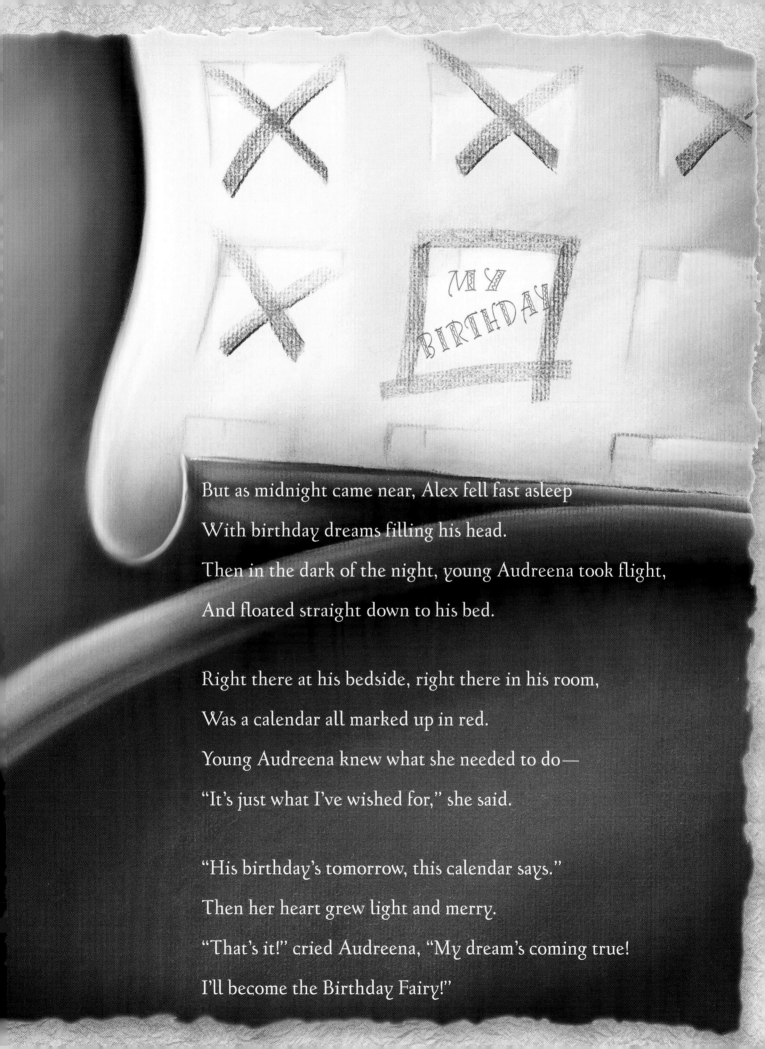

But as midnight came near, Alex fell fast asleep

With birthday dreams filling his head.

Then in the dark of the night, young Audreena took flight,

And floated straight down to his bed.

Right there at his bedside, right there in his room,

Was a calendar all marked up in red.

Young Audreena knew what she needed to do—

"It's just what I've wished for," she said.

"His birthday's tomorrow, this calendar says."

Then her heart grew light and merry.

"That's it!" cried Audreena, "My dream's coming true!

I'll become the Birthday Fairy!"

"I must tell my father; I must tell him right now.

I'm sure that he'll understand."

Then suddenly Alden appeared to Audreena,

Reaching out and touching her hand.

"Audreena, my child, you've discovered your dream.

I'm so proud that you didn't give up.

I now have a gift that I've saved just for you."

Then he brought out a golden cup.

"I've something to give you; right here in this cup.

It's stardust from your baby hair.

It holds the power to grant children's desires.

So sprinkle it all with great care."

With a kiss for good luck, and her magical cup,

Audreena had much work to do.

Before the day breaks and before Alex wakes,

She must make his wishes come true.

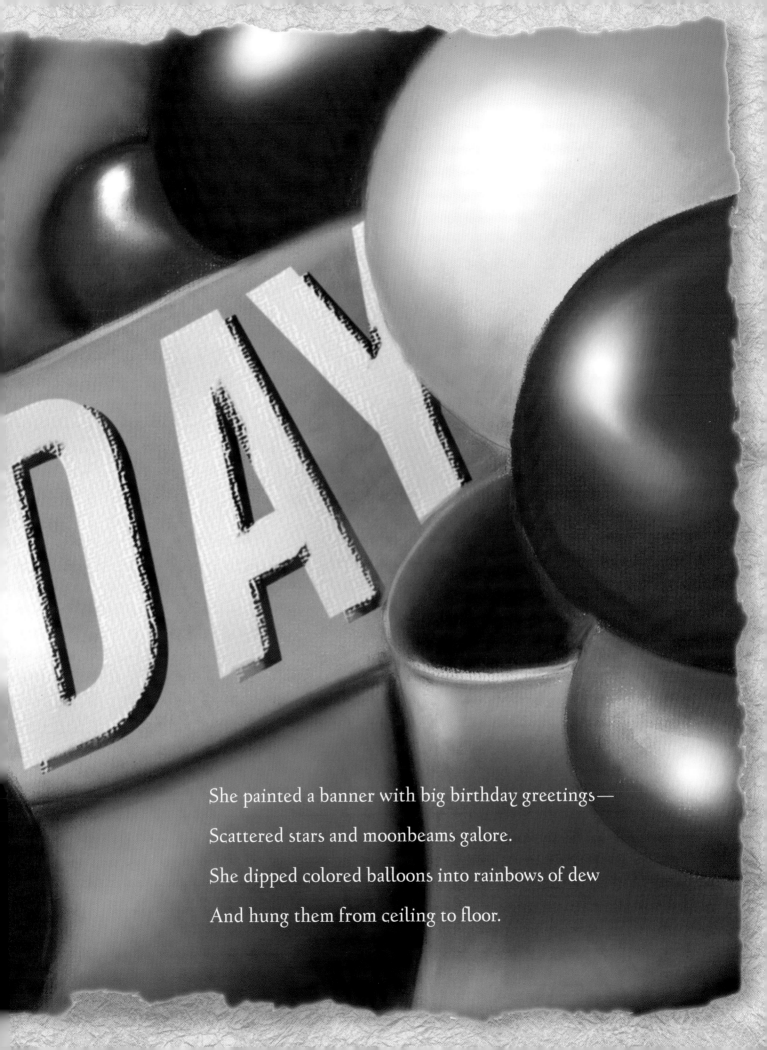

She painted a banner with big birthday greetings—

Scattered stars and moonbeams galore.

She dipped colored balloons into rainbows of dew

And hung them from ceiling to floor.

She speckled his room with dots of confetti.

And strung streamers all over the wall.

Then she sprinkled the stardust on Alex's heart

For the loveliest gift of them all:

The feelings of sadness in Alex's heart

Were replaced by feelings of joy.

He knew that his parents could never forget

The birthday of their little boy.

When Alex awoke and he opened his eyes,

He smiled and laughed right away.

"Mom and Dad, come quick! Just look at my room!

You didn't forget my birthday!"

When his parents came in, they both stared in delight.

It seemed like a wonderful dream.

Then they saw the bright glow in young Alex's eyes,

And his happiness made them both beam.

Alex looked for his tooth tucked under his pillow.

Instead, he discovered a note.

It glittered and glowed with a sparkling dust,

And these words that Audreena wrote:

"Dearest Alex my friend,
you're a wonderful boy.

"I'm happy your birthday is here.

If you like this surprise, please send me a smile;

And I'll visit you year after year."

Alex held the note close, then gave a big smile

And a bright light lit up the sky.

Then it rose from the earth to the cloud up above,

And all of the fairies knew why.

For Audreena had found all her hopes and her dreams,

And made all of her wishes come true.

And so starting today and from this day on

She'll be the Birthday Fairy for you!

Audreena
the Birthday Fairy

Created by the Editors of Creative Publishing international, Inc., in cooperation with Birthday Fairy, Inc. The Birthday Fairy is a trademark of Birthday Fairy, Inc. and is used under license.

Writer: Stephanie Sample

Contributing Editor: Susan M. Riley

Illustrator: Scott Sample

5900 Green Oak Drive
Minnetonka, Minnesota 55343
1-800-328-3895
www.howtobookstore.com

President/CEO: David D. Murphy

Vice President/Editorial: Patricia K. Jacobsen

Vice President/Retail Sales and Marketing: Richard M. Miller

Vice President/Custom Publishing: Hugh J. Kennedy

Project Editor: Jackie Anderson

Library of Congress Cataloging-in-Publication Data

First Edition. 2000
ISBN: 0-86573-485-2

Printed in Singapore